WHERE IT ALL BEGAN ...

A TAMSIN KERNICK ENGLISH COZY MYSTERY

BOOK 0

LUCY EMBLEM

CHAPTER ONE

As the taxi wound between the magnificent Malvern Hills - right in the heart of England - Tamsin balanced her suitcase on her lap and gazed open-mouthed at the views opening up before her.

"See this big gap we're driving through?" said the chatty driver as they passed through a cutting with the rock rearing up to a great height either side of them.

"It feels so ancient!" said Tamsin, all agog.

"It's called the Wyche Cutting. And do you know why it's called Wyche?" He was clearly one of those knowledgeable taxi-drivers who loves to give their rides a guided tour.

"Did witches live here?" she suggested tentatively.

"Nah!" he laughed, delighted to be able to show off his knowledge. "It's from the Saxon. Old English, you know. Ancient. It's to do with transporting salt."

"Salt?"

"Yep. This is an Iron Age salt route. Salt was valuable in those days, you know."

"I had no idea .." Her voice tailed off as the vista right across Herefordshire to Wales opened up before her. "This is amazing - and so different from what I'm used to in Birmingham!"

They'd been climbing all the way from the railway station in Great Malvern, and were still going up.

"Here you are, West Malvern!" said the jolly driver, and they turned off the main road and went through a couple of hairpin bends, zigzagging steeply up the hill till they came to a stop above a long low house. The driveway overlooked the house, and she could see the grass growing on the roof as she looked across the top of the building to take in the view once more.

The driver jumped out, stretched noisily, and opened her door, ready to take her suitcase for her. As she stepped out Tamsin could see how far up the Hills they were - it looked as though you could step out from the house right onto the many footpaths that she could see weaving across the hill above her. She savoured the unaccustomed silence: she could hear some distant baa-ing, and a strange mewing she couldn't recognise - of a circling buzzard calling out to its mate, slowly drifting on a thermal as its astonishingly sharp eyes hunted the pastures and scrub for its next meal.

Her thoughts were interrupted by a flurry of deep barking, then two big black labradors raced up to the gate, tails wagging furiously, tongues lolling, mobbing her with the friendliest of greetings. She fished in her pocket and pulled out a note to pay her taxi, saying "Keep the change!" in a grand gesture that she hoped she wouldn't regret, her funds already being at a very low level - hence the need for her to take this house-sitting job for the next two months.

"Ow! Your tails hurt!" she laughed, as she stepped through the gate with her suitcase, two thick tails whacking her legs and drumming on her case as she negotiated the steep steps down to the house. The taxi driver did a several-point turn in the narrow driveway and, giving her a cheery wave, he drove away. Tamsin realised her adventure had truly begun.

"Come in, come in, come in," she heard a voice from the open kitchen door. "Dogs, leave her alone!"

"Oh, they're fine - just getting to know me," she answered politely, taking the last step and peering from the sunny garden into the dark kitchen to get a glimpse of her new employer.

A small wiry figure with pepper-and-salt hair and beard emerged from the depths of the kitchen, wiping his hands on a tea-towel before abruptly extending a hand to her, nearly jabbing her in the midriff.

"Robin Langley-Fortescue. Robin. And you're Tamsin? Good good good. I see you've met the horrors."

"What are their names?"

"The one with the frilly ear is Flora. She caught it on barbed wire up on the Hills, years ago. And this bigger one is Jasper. They're brother and sister, same age. And they egg each other on in their naughtiness ..." He suddenly remembered himself and added, "but they're good dogs really - no trouble. You'll enjoy them, I hope. Seeing as your references said how much you like animals?"

"Oh I do! And I'm sure I will enjoy them! You'll have to show me where everything is, what to feed them and all that."

"I expect you'd like a cup of tea first? How was your journey?"

"Oh, it was fine - Birmingham is a bit nearer than the Arctic," she laughed, "so just a hop for you, I'm sure!"

"You're right! I'm used to trekking thousands of miles over snowy wastes." He waved his arm expansively. "I can tell you there were times when I could have done with a comfy inter-city train!" he guffawed loudly and turned away.

They adjourned to the living room, with its enormous picture-window showing as much of the view as possible - a feature Tamsin would learn was common to many of the houses on this side of the Malvern Hills, who enjoyed glorious sunsets while their neighbours on the other side of the Hills were in shade from early in the afternoon.

"Do you take sugar?" yelled her host as he clattered cups in the kitchen.

"No thank you," replied Tamsin distractedly, as she looked at all the black and white photos on the walls, of snow, snow, and more snow. Sometimes there was a smiling person clad in furs - some local scout, she guessed. Occasionally a tent could be seen, and some dogs and sledges.

"Ah, you've seen what I do!" said Robin. Those were taken .. on a number of expeditions. Lots of them," he grinned, "Lots ..." and placed the tea tray on the table and offered Tamsin her tea and a seat. She was quick to put her mug down on a nearby shelf, as two black noses jogged her elbow and by lurching forward she just managed not to spill the lot on the Persian carpet.

"They'll calm down in a moment," said Robin nervously, and perhaps seeing that he was in danger of losing his house-sitter before she'd even begun, roared, "DOGS!"

They both froze, looked sideways at him, and slunk away to their beds in the kitchen.

"That's better! We'll get a bit of peace now. You don't train dogs by any chance, do you?" he asked hopefully.

"I used to enjoy doing 'showjumping' in the back garden with my Jack Russell," she smiled. "They weren't real jumps of course - just bamboo canes laid across flowerpots - I was about 7 or 8 I think. But we had fun! Perhaps you'd like me to take the dogs to classes while I'm here?"

"Oh, I'm sure that's not necessary. But don't let them get away with anything. Give 'em an inch and they'll take a mile," he smiled broadly, coughed, and sat back in his armchair. "Let's get all the details out of the way," and they fell to confirming their terms, payment details, and dates. He gave her a sheet of paper with phone numbers on - for the vet, a neighbour, doctor, and so on. Amongst the numbers was one heavily scratched out. As she looked at it, Robin snatched back the sheet and put it on the table saying, "It'll be here for you. Let's hope you never need it! Let me show you what you may need to water in the garden." And they set off for a tour of the lovely garden, with a central lawn scattered with chewed up tennis balls and other dog toys, and wild-looking trees and bushes all around the house, with a cottage garden effect of chaotic colour in the flower-beds. At the bottom of the garden was a robust fence, protecting residents from the sheer drop to the neighbour below.

On asking about the dogs, he took her to the kitchen where he showed her where their food was, their bowls, beds and so on. The clattering of the bowls aroused great interest in the dogs. But they were sadly disappointed to see them parked back in the cupboard again.

"Where are their leads?"

"Oh we don't use leads. Just step out of the gate and straight on to the Hills. They don't run off .. much."

Tamsin resolved to fashion leads out of rope till she could get to a shop to buy two. She had a slight sinking feeling in her stomach over what she'd committed to - hadn't she heard sheep bleating when she arrived? Getting the dogs shot while their owner was away was definitely not on her agenda.

"I'll be leaving tomorrow," he nodded his head towards the row of suitcases and awkward-shaped bags stacked up in front of the fireplace. "So we can eat together this evening, if that's alright with you?"

Tamsin nodded dutifully.

"You can finish off whatever perishable food is in the kitchen - tide you over till you get out to the shops, don't you know."

Tamsin finished her tea and went to unpack, 'helped' by Flora and Jasper, who found her belongings irresistible. She had to chase after Jasper twice to retrieve an item of underwear that she didn't want trailed all round the house.

From her bedroom window she could see the Hills climbing steeply to the right, and to the left - part of the vista across to Wales. "I don't think I'll tire of this view in a hurry!" she said to her appreciative audience.

At last she sat on the bed, two drooly muzzles on her knee. She sighed and was glad she'd noticed a washing machine in the kitchen. It would clearly be getting a lot of use! Picking up her phone, she whizzed off a text to her mother:

> *Arrived safe and sound. Nice dogs. Strange man - glad he's off tomorrow. Beautiful place! Think I'll get very fit here, up and down these hills. Talk soon xxx*

Tossing the phone on the bed, she picked up the book conveniently left on her bedside table. Not a Gideon Bible, but clearly a bible of a different kind - *Surviving in the Arctic by Renowned Explorer Robin Langley-Fortescue,* she read, and there was a smiling Robin, wrapped in a parka with a massive fur-lined hood, his pepper-and-salt beard frosted from his freezing breath. In the background there was miles of snow. "Whatever floats your boat," she mumbled to the dogs. "I prefer rain to snow any day. And I guess with the Welsh Mountains just over there, we'll get plenty of rain here!" Two black tails whacked the bed rhythmically in response. "And I also guess I'm becoming a mad dog-lady, talking to you like this?"

She could have sworn the dogs were smiling as their brown eyes gazed into hers, and she felt something twang in her heart.

CHAPTER TWO

At supper that evening, after supervising her feeding the dogs, Robin filled her in on a few details. She noticed that there were dozens of copies of his book - in piles round the living room; in the airing cupboard when she went to fetch a towel; stacked on top of the bookshelves.

"I guess you're very famous from your book?" she ventured.

"Ah, yes. Um. You could say that. I get invited to do lots of talks, you know, with slides. Harks back to the days of lantern slides when explorers would come back and enlighten the populace about the wonders of the world!" He laughed loudly. "Of course these days it's all electronic slideshows, and people are much more knowledgeable about the world from seeing it all on television. But they love to actually meet the explorer."

He leant forward and refilled his wine-glass, Tamsin having sensibly put a hand over her own. "I have to turn up looking as though I've just parked my team of huskies outside the hall," he laughed nervously. "They expect me to look the part, fur parka, boots, and all. Gets very hot, I have to say ..."

"I had a quick look at your book - I will read it all, of course! - and I see it's mostly about your very first expedition, back in the day."

"Long time ago now, it's true. And my publishers are absolutely *clamouring* for a sequel. Apparently a second book boosts the sales of the first one, once the author starts sitting on those tv sofas, signing books, and whatnot." His eyes went round the room, noting all the books, "And I could certainly do with a boost in sales ..."

"Is it hard thinking of something new to write, when you put so much into the first book?"

"I think you've hit the nail on the head there, young lady! But it's what the public want, apparently."

"I hope you've packed a pen and paper!"

He twitched and laughed again.

"I bet you have to take lots of photos too - wouldn't colour ones work better? I imagine brilliant blue skies .."

"Oh yes, plenty of camera equipment," he said, eying the heap of packed bags of all shapes and sizes. "More wine!" and he sloshed another load of wine into his glass, Tamsin picking up her own glass for a sip and gently shaking her head.

"Time for you to tell me about yourself! *Tamsin Kernick* ... isn't that a Cornish name?"

"You're right, it is! My mother is a great romantic and spent her teenage years reading love stories. She loved the ones set in the coves and beaches of Cornwall, so when she met a real live Cornishman she married him without delay."

"And gave you a Cornish name!"

"Not many people know that - but I suppose with your inquisitive mind you pick up interesting snippets everywhere! You're right, Tamsin's the Cornish diminutive for Thomasina. Glad she didn't give me that mouthful for a handle!"

"Lovely name - in either form." He took another glug of wine and smiled at her - or was it a leer? "So you're not actually *from* Cornwall?"

"No. Though we've spent plenty of summer holidays there, what with Dad's cousins all still living there. It's very wild round the coast. Whereas the landscape here seems ... more civilised somehow."

"Don't be deceived! The weather can get quite wild and woolly here too. It can change dramatically pretty quickly up on the Beacons. You can watch the rain sweeping across the land on its way in from the Welsh mountains, the Black Mountains - so-called because they always look dark from this side, specially when it's raining!" he laughed, and unsteadily drained the wine bottle into his glass. "So what decided you to venture south to West Malvern?"

"I couldn't settle to anything really - I knew I didn't want to go on studying. My parents are all for me finding a nice local boy and settling down in the same area for the rest of my days. But that didn't feel right. So I decided to try something completely different, in a different place."

"Something completely different in a different place," he repeated back to her. "I think that's a really wise decision, young Tamsin."

There was a pause while they both thought on this.

"What time do you go tomorrow?"

"Taxi booked for half past seven. Just time for a full English breakfast before I set off."

"Then we'd better clear away and let you get some beauty sleep!" Tamsin stood and carried some plates to the kitchen, running some hot water into a bowl to wash up.

"They'll need another wee before bed," said Robin as he tottered into the kitchen, banging into the door-frame.

"Ok. Look, I can deal with all of this - perhaps you need to head to bed?"

"Reckon you're right," he said as he looked appraisingly at her. "Lucky dogs," he added, as he left the kitchen.

Shortly afterwards, Tamsin settled the dogs in the kitchen and took herself to bed. She looked at the keyhole of her bedroom door: no key. So, in a moment of mild panic - which she justified to herself as sensible caution - she wedged the chair against the door-handle. She'd be glad when she had the house to herself.

CHAPTER THREE

The night passed without incident, and Tamsin had taken the hint and was up at 6.30 wielding a frying pan to produce the full English breakfast Robin had mentioned.

He didn't look much the worse for wear for all his drinking the night before, and he was busy checking over his bags and making sure he had his travel documents handy.

"Where are you flying to?" Tamsin reached out a hand as he picked up the ticket wallet. He quickly stowed it in his breast pocket.

"Ahh, there are a few stops and changes. You can't fly direct to the North Pole, you know!" he laughed his jerky laugh. "Here - don't burn the bacon," he said, and lifting the lid of the teapot, peered inside it. "This ready to pour?"

Tamsin watched him plough through the massive breakfast as she nursed her mug of tea.

"Not eating?"

"I don't eat breakfast," she smiled. "I'll take the dogs out and start exploring once you've gone. Work up an appetite for lunch. Then maybe I'll head over to town this afternoon and find out what's what."

"Good good good. All good. Hope you'll like it here. Plenty to see in

Malvern. If you feel fit enough you could get a bike and explore all the little villages round here. Ledbury's a quaint old town, lots of black-and-white half-timbered houses. There's the River Severn, of course, Little Malvern's a wonderful place ..."

"I hadn't thought of a bike. That's a great idea!"

"There's a good bike shop in town. Very popular round here, cycling - they like the challenge of all these hills - super fit. Everywhere you go is either steep up or steep down. You can see the lights of the mountain bikes swooping over the Hills at night sometimes." He tipped his head towards the Hills above them, though they couldn't actually see them from the house, as it was built into the side of the hill and most of the windows faced West. He lavished butter on another slice of toast. "As I said, you'll need to be fit. They ran the Tour de France through here a few years ago. You should see the speed they zipped up and over the Hill! Gone by in a jiffy. I'm fit - with all that tramping about in the snow, of course," he laughed nervously, "and they made me feel tired to see them whistle past!"

"I'll be a shadow of myself when you come back," laughed Tamsin, "with all this exercise!" She looked at the clock and quickly ran through the dogs' timetable again, checking she had the list of important phone numbers to hand.

Flora and Jasper suddenly started off barking, racing up and down the path to make sure everyone knew that the taxi had arrived.

Tamsin clapped her hand to her head, "Hey, where's the house key?"

"Oh yes, key ... here you go." Robin fished in his pocket and handed over the big bunch of keys, as Tamsin slowly shook her head in wonder, wondering what she would have done had the key gone to the North Pole with Robin. Pocketing the key, she followed him to the gate, bringing a couple of the smaller bags with her. She was surprised at how light they were. She had thought that everything you needed on an Arctic expedition, from snow boots to cans of food, would be heavy. But judging by the way the driver swung the bags easily into the taxi, none of them appeared to be.

Eventually all was loaded, and Tamsin stood at the gate with the dogs and waved Robin off as the taxi zigzagged back down the steep hill.

"It's just us now, kids," she said with a sigh, and noted the loosening of her shoulders, and the relief she felt now her employer was gone.

"Let's find you some leads," and she headed to the garden shed to hunt for some rope.

CHAPTER FOUR

The shed had a big padlock on it. Fishing the bunch of keys from her pocket, she tried all the likely ones and at last heard the lock click open.

"Let's see what we can find, guys," she told her waggy friends as she stepped into the old wooden building. Like so many sheds, this one was crammed with all manner of stuff - gardening tools, lawnmower, paint pots, old warped cardboard boxes with dirty flowerpots and faded seed packets, cans of weedkiller and fertiliser, skis .. Skis? "And here are some old ski-boots too," she pointed them out to Flora whose nose was sniffing busily at everything. "Doesn't Robin need skis where he's going? Oh, perhaps these are old, and he picks up some modern equipment when he gets there. That makes sense." She continued searching and chattering to the dogs, "Ah, here's some fine rope, climbing rope - that'll do nicely! Don't want you two making a monkey of me on our first day."

Once she'd fashioned two leads - she'd always enjoyed Art and Crafts at school, and the rope felt much softer once it was plaited - they set off up the hill. It didn't seem so steep ascending it, as both dogs hauled her with all their might. "Steady boys! Sorry - girl and boy," she said as they pulled ahead of her. Maybe those training classes would be a good idea ...

She was too nervous to let the dogs off lead once she got up to the top of the Hills - despite Robin's assurances. There were plenty of sheep and lambs about, unfenced. "Play safe till you know your enemy!" she said to herself, as she delighted in the antics of the young lambs, hurtling about in gangs, jumping on their mothers' backs, generally behaving like young-sters everywhere.

She turned her steps south and followed the crest of the Hills. There were a few walkers out, looking well-equipped for their hike in colourful jackets, some with walking poles. "Don't think I can manage those as well as two tangled leads," she laughed to her charges, who had their noses firmly on the ground the whole time, forgetting she even existed.

She heard that mewing sound again and wondered what it was - something between a peep and a mew. She spotted a man with a camera on a tripod - a birdwatcher? - and wandered over to see if he was friendly. Flora and Jasper were both sufficiently tired by now to take the opportu-nity to lie down, enabling her to speak to the man. He was friendly, and another of those who love to teach.

"Look down there," he pointed down the side of the hill where they could see a large bird of prey hovering below them. "Keep watching, he's about to dive ..." and sure enough, after a couple of minutes of the Buzzard hovering first in one place, then darting to another and hovering again, the bird suddenly turned into an air-to-ground missile and hurtled down to catch the vole or beetle or whatever it was whose tiny move-ments had caught its eye.

Tamsin was enthralled, and already beginning to fall in love with this new place with its friendly people, this new life - and even these new dogs, trying though they were! After a couple of hours she was back 'home' and munching her way hungrily through lunch. Cans of things were really not her chosen diet, so after a brief period to recover, she took a shopping bag and set off to trek through the Wyche Cutting to Great Malvern.

Two hours later, her shopping bag full of fresh food and some deli-cious-looking bread from the bakery, as well as two smart new leads - one pink and one blue so she'd know which dog was in which hand - she found a cosy-looking café and sagged gratefully into a comfy armchair by the window.

"You would like *un café,* yes?" Tamsin turned to see a slim, dark man with bushy black eyebrows, one of which was arched up as a question.

"Oh yes please, I'm exhausted!"

"You are new here, *n'est-ce pas?* I have not met you before. I am Jean-Philippe. Welcome to The Cake Stop - *bienvenue!*"

"Hello Jean-Philippe! Or should I say *Bonjour?* I'm Tamsin. I've walked miles today, a coffee would be a life-saver."

"Then may I show you what we have to offer?" He turned and waved his arm expansively towards the counter where the large coffee machinery shone invitingly behind the cake shelves. "You can leave your shopping there on the chair, it'll be fine."

Tamsin was stunned by the huge array of sumptuous-looking cakes, and treated herself to a large slice of carrot cake and a Cappuccino. And as she sat and tucked into the moist, delicious, cake, enjoying the ambience with its quiet music - just enough to keep conversations private without drowning them out - she realised what a find this café was, with its sleek black tables, comfy armchairs, and friendly host.

She wasn't to know then how large this café would figure in her life for the next many years!

CHAPTER FIVE

A few days later, Robin rang up.

"Hello? Can you hear me?" he shouted. "I'm just transferring to another region and hit civilisation. Thought I should check in with you. Can you hear me?" he shouted again.

Tamsin could hear him as clear as a bell - which surprised her a little, as she would expect a call from the Arctic wastes to be a bit more challenging, at least a bit crackly.

She reassured him that everything was just fine, the dogs were fine, the house was fine, the weather was even fine.

"Glad to hear it," he shouted, "heavy snow here, of course - oh, gotta go," he added as he rang off, but not before Tamsin heard the bing-bong typical of airport announcements. Her vision of a shack on the snow with a little bi-plane parked beside it was shattered. Very puzzling. Maybe he was still in Norway, obviously a civilised country with all amenities. That's what it must be.

She dismissed her worries and fetched the pink and blue leads for the dogs' morning outing. They wagged their solid tails eagerly, whacking her leg and the kitchen cabinets with equal force. And when they'd ascended the North Hill, as Tamsin had discovered it to be called, and turned toward the Worcestershire Beacon - another place she'd learnt - it became clear the sheep had been moved.

"Ok, guys, time to see just how well you behave," and she unclipped the leads. As soon as they'd set off she tried calling them back - "Flora! Jasper!" and they actually turned and came trotting back. So Tamsin strolled along the path without a care in the world, and everything went just fine .. for a few hundred yards.

Suddenly a small brown animal like a dog, jumped out from behind a gorse bush just in front of Jasper, and took off down the slope, both Flora and Jasper instantly in hot pursuit. She gasped and yelled - but to no avail. The dogs were hurtling at speed and nothing was going to stop them!

.. until they arrived at the edge of a quarry. The animal they were chasing, who was fast stretching out ahead of them, disappeared into a clump of ancient trees clinging to the side of the hill, and the two dogs, panting hard, pulled up at the fenced edge of the sheer drop.

Tamsin was scrambling down the hill behind them, her heart in her mouth. "Oh my God," she said, as with trembling fingers she re-attached the leads, not noticing in her haste that Flora had the blue lead and Jasper was now resplendent in pink. "Oh my God!" she gasped again, patting her heart, as a couple of walkers emerged from the clump of trees.

"That Muntjac give you a run for your money?" the young man asked with a laugh. And seeing Tamsin's baffled face, added, "It's a deer, little solitary things. Bit of a pest really. Not like native deer."

"Are you alright?" asked the girl, "You look awfully pale."

"Had a shock," stammered Tamsin. "They're not my dogs, you see. I was told they were safe to let off lead. But I'm ok now, thanks!" she smiled and headed up the hill again, her dogs firmly on their leads, albeit the wrong ones.

And that's when the decision was made to enrol both dogs in classes.

"You two need to learn some manners," she admonished them as she puffed her way up the hill, the dogs walking noticeably more slowly now. "I'll find out the nearest class, and you're going!"

CHAPTER SIX

To say Tamsin was disappointed with the classes was an understatement. Held in a wet field full of agitated, barking dogs, a short bus journey outside the town, the man who took the class was brash and loud and only got results by yanking a dog's lead and browbeating both dog and owner - who felt too embarrassed to object.

There were about twenty dogs in the class - it was noisy, chaotic, and she learnt nothing, except that shouting and bullying was no way to deal with a fellow creature, especially one who was on a lead and had no escape. She resolved to find a better way.

So, being Tamsin, she took matters into her own hands. Cycling to the Library the next day, she found a number of books which seemed to show a kinder approach to dog training - in fact, many of them actually explained what was going on in the dog's head, an area of total mystery to the nasty instructor she'd been paying.

She took as many as she was allowed back home with her, and a new world began to open up before her.

"It's amazing what you guys can do, other than stuffing your faces and chasing things," she told her charges as she read of the wonders that dogs could learn and do well - dancing, search and rescue, agility, and more. "You're going to turn over a new leaf!"

And so she set to with lessons. Flora learnt a bit faster than Jasper did, but once they both found that sausages were involved, they became keen students, and actually became much more responsive. Tamsin enjoyed having discovered the Library, which seemed to be a centre for all kinds of community events. And on one visit after she had chosen some more dog books, she browsed the noticeboard. As so often, there was a shortage of drawing pins, and several items were piled up under the same pin. Poking around, through sheer nosiness, she found at the bottom of one pile a tattered flyer titled *Arctic Exploration: a lecture,* bearing the photo of Robin Langley-Fortescue with his frosted snowy beard. She snatched the sheet off the board and wandered over to the desk.

"Do you have any books about this person?" she asked the Librarian, who went to her computer to investigate. A small elderly lady who was piling her returned books onto the desk leant across and peered at the flyer in Tamsin's hand.

"Oh yes, that's our local explorer!" she said. "Quite the mystery man ..."

"Mystery man?" Tamsin enquired, as pieces began to fall into place.

"For all his eccentricities, I think he has his head very well screwed on."

"Tell me more! My name's Tamsin, by the way, Tamsin Kernick."

"Happily, my dear! I'm Charity Cleveland," and moving her glasses to her other hand, her bony hand clasped Tamsin's hand warmly. "I'm about finished here and I'm just going to get a coffee - care to join me?"

Tamsin didn't need to hear a coffee invitation twice, and gathering their newly-borrowed books and Tamsin pushing her new bike, they headed to The Cake Stop where they were warmly welcomed by Jean-Philippe - who evidently knew Charity very well - and settled down to talk about the "mystery man".

"I have to explain," started Tamsin, "I'm actually minding Mr. Langley-Fortescue's house for a while. And his dogs. That's why I was at the

Library researching - they're so badly behaved I decided to take on the project of teaching them some manners while I'm with them."

"Oh, that sounds such fun! I love dogs. My little old Crumpet died last year - I do miss her so."

"Oh, I'm sorry to hear that .." began Tamsin.

"So I have a new puppy booked! I'm going to call her Muffin."

"That's exciting! I'm just learning about teaching puppies - what they need to learn first, sort of thing," she patted her bag full of books.

"Muffin's arriving next week - perhaps you can teach me?"

And so the two women got off to a famous start. And as they worked their way through their coffee and the inevitable cake, Charity told Tamsin more about Robin.

"I've been to a couple of his lectures down the years, you see, and I've got a very good memory - grey hair, but the brainbox is still working well," she smiled pleasantly as she tapped her head. "And I recognised a lot of the pictures he showed us. They were the same ones. Identical."

"But don't all snowy wastes look the same?"

"I'd expect him to have a new jacket on his third or fourth expedition."

"That's a point ..."

"And I wouldn't expect him to use the exact same dog to lead his sledge. One of them had a very unusual colour pattern. And there it was, six years later. Same dog."

"So what you're saying is ..."

"I'm not sure how much our explorer actually explores. Now," she added, seeing Tamsin's jaw drop, "you can't quote me on that. It's just a thought in my head. I don't actually care whether he goes to the North Pole or not, but I do like to know what makes people tick, and I wonder why he feels the need to perpetuate this explorer image."

"Wow. Just wow." Tamsin thought of the lightweight baggage, the skis, the strange phone call, "What you're saying makes everything else fit into place. So he's deluding everyone over his expeditions - you think?"

"I think it highly likely that he's deluding himself."

"This is rather alarming. I think I'd better be ready to leave the day he returns. Do you think he's bats?"

"As in dangerous? No. I really don't think so. He reminds me of a boy I was at school with - always telling tall stories to make himself look good. Of course no-one believed any of them. But he was harmless. He became a care assistant for old people," she gazed into the distance - this elderly lady who clearly didn't consider herself old, "They probably share far-fetched stories together!"

"I have to say there are a few things that just don't seem to add up," Tamsin said thoughtfully. "But he does like his dogs, in his way. They're pretty well looked after. Just naughty!"

"I don't think you have anything to worry about, my dear. But here - this is my phone number - I've got one of these modern phones you can write messages with!" she fished in her large bag and waved her mobile triumphantly, perched her glasses on her nose as she leant her head back to read her own number out to Tamsin, who tapped it into her phone.

"Oh, now my phone's buzzing!" Charity jumped. "What have I done?"

"I've just sent you a message," laughed Tamsin. "Now you've got my number too!"

"Extraordinary ..." Charity peered at her screen. "How will I find it again?"

"May I?" Tamsin reached for her phone, and quickly showed her how to add her number to her contacts, and how to find her contacts again next time.

"You young people are so clever with these gadgets - thank you, dear."

"I'd just love to meet Muffin as soon as she arrives! Will you call me? We'll have fun teaching her."

And Tamsin cycled back round the Hills, knowing that she had made a firm friendship - though she had no idea at that time how large this friend was going to loom in her life!

CHAPTER SEVEN

Tamsin couldn't get enough of her studying. She loved it, and she loved trying everything out with Jasper and Flora, delighting in their individual responses and personalities. She could be quite boisterous with Jasper when playing with him with a toy - a great way to teach him to retrieve and release politely, she'd discovered - but had to be a bit milder with Flora, who could get worried easily. And so she started to learn the nuances of training different individual dogs.

Occasionally there was a postcard from Robin, posted at some airport or other foreign place with an unrecognisable name. Her days were passing peacefully and her time in West Malvern would be coming to a close in a few weeks. She was loving it here, and thought a lot about what she was going to do with herself at the end of the two months. What could she do to earn money? She kept asking herself this question, but so far hadn't come up with an answer.

She'd just finished an active game with the two dogs in the garden one day, when she came in to find the phone ringing.

"Darling! Are you his latest?" asked a woman rather drunkenly when she answered.

"Er, Mr.Langley-Fortescue is away on an expedition at the moment, I'm afraid. Can I take a message?"

The woman caller laughed uproariously, snorted, and ended the call abruptly.

"Well dogs, that's a bit odd, isn't it?"

The dogs, panting from their game, showed little interest in the phone call and sighed as they subsided onto their beds.

Tamsin put the call from her mind and after lunch set off with the dogs for a long tramp on the Hills, incorporating some of the training she'd been working on. She'd just finished a session with a few recalls, pleased with the dogs' speedy response, put them back on their pink and blue leads and started to walk forward together comfortably, without the dogs pulling her arms out of their sockets.

"Excuse me!" a woman's voice called from behind her. Tamsin turned to find a middle-aged couple, with a Spaniel - his nose to the ground - hauling the woman along. "Sorry to bother you, but we were watching you. Hope you don't mind!"

"Not at all!" smiled Tamsin.

"Only, we were awfully impressed with your dogs, weren't we Brian? I expect you've been training them for years!"

"Actually, they're not mine - I'm just doing a bit of work with them."

"How long have you been training them?"

"Oh, just a few weeks," she replied airily.

The couple turned and stared at each other in astonishment. "What can you do with our Flash?" asked Brian.

Tamsin asked Jasper and Flora to lie down, dropped the leads, and reached for Flash's lead. In a few moments she'd got Flash hanging on her every word, greatly helped with the tiny morsels of cheese she paid him in return.

"Oh my!" exclaimed Brian as Tamsin handed the lead back to him and picked up the Labradors' leads, "That's amazing. Would you give us lessons? We'll pay, of course!"

"We did go to classes once," added the lady, "but I just didn't like what they were doing to poor Flash, so we left. But you're just lovely with him!"

"We don't shout at each other when we want something, so there's no need to shout at dogs either," Tamsin agreed.

And after some more magic phone-number-exchanging with them, having fixed a day for their first lesson Tamsin floated down North Hill on a cloud of joy, and a realisation that this was something she could do!

CHAPTER EIGHT

Tamsin's lessons with Flash were getting noticed, not least because she made sure she was near the path when she worked him, and before the week was out she had two more students. One was a neighbour of Brian's and the other had come via Charity, who was delighting in how well baby Muffin was doing. Using commonsense, compassion, and some tips from one of the books, Charity was enjoying a full night's sleep with the puppy after only three days.

And this is when Tamsin realised that everyone knew Charity! She was one of those friendly, helpful, and approachable people who had been around for ever, knew everyone, and was always ready to help. So she was the obvious person to ask about lodgings for when Tamsin's house-sitting stay was over.

Two phone calls was all it had taken for Tamsin to get fixed up with Dorothy, one of Charity's friends, with a very modest rent in return for teaching her resident dog Eddie not to steal food.

"Thank you so much, Charity, this is such fun!" Tamsin enthused to her friend, as they took their places at a table with comfy armchairs in the window at The Cake Stop. Charity placed little Muffin carefully on her lap, and beamed with pride over her puppy.

"Well, you're really good at it, my dear," responded Charity, who despite her bird-like size was shovelling spoonfuls of sugar into her tea.

"I had no idea - it seems to be a gift. I just understand the dogs. I really think I've fallen on my feet," Tamsin smiled happily. "I think I'll be able to make a go of this."

Jean-Philippe ambled over to greet his customers. "Ah, *un petit chiot!*" and he leant forward to touch the little puppy's back, as Muffin wagged her tail vigorously. "And what news from the Arctic, *hein?*"

"I haven't heard recently, though I got a postcard about three weeks ago."

Jean-Philippe perched on the arm of a vacant armchair. "I went to one of his lectures once. Not for me! The pictures all looked the same - one flat snowy scene after another. Someone in an anorak waving. All those expeditions to the same place - surely it is boring when all you see is snow?"

"Not my cup of tea either," nodded Tamsin, "but each to his own, I suppose."

"I imagine it won't be long before he's back?"

"Quite soon, yes."

"And you? What are you going to do then, Tamsin?"

"I'm staying! I love it here - you've got another blow-in!"

"*Ah oui*, but I am a blow-in myself! You maybe guessed from my accent ..." he winked. "And what will you do?"

"I'm going to train dogs - kindly."

"I will do my best to tell anybody who comes here with a dog."

"That's terrific, thank you! And I wonder ... I'll need an indoor space to run classes. You wouldn't know of anywhere, would you?"

Jean-Philippe started to shake his head mournfully, then stopped suddenly and said, "*Mais oui!* I have an idea!"

Charity and Tamsin leant forward eagerly.

"I have a friend who runs the dance club - it's always closed in the daytime. I wonder ..."

"Could you ask him?"

"I will do that. I will ask him. He may be glad of *un peu d'argent.*"

"I hope he doesn't want too much *argent* - I don't have much ..."

"He is a friend. I will ask him," and so saying, he turned back to the counter where a queue of backpackers had appeared, their backpacks swinging dangerously behind them as they chatted. "I go and rescue the cake display." He raised his bushy black eyebrows and went to serve his customers, while Tamsin, thrilled with her new home and possibly a new venue for her classes, contentedly played with little Muffin.

CHAPTER NINE

It was her last week of house-sitting before Robin was due to return, and Tamsin thought she'd better catch up with some housework. She was a reasonably tidy person, but she hadn't done much in the way of cleaning, so she got out the antiquated hoover and some dusters and polish she found in the broom cupboard, and set to.

The big bookshelves were tricky to dust, as there were so many books crammed in, and little ornaments and bits and bobs that Robin had collected on his travels. She came across an old shoe-box, and her curiosity got the better of her. Opening it up, she found loads of slides - transparencies as she believed they were called. Holding them up to the light, she saw snow, snow, and more snow. These looked like the images in Robin's book. Some had writing on, and most were dated fourteen years ago. She replaced the box carefully, and continued dusting, keeping a careful eye out for any further stores of photos.

But she found none. No more slides, no colour prints, nothing. She shrugged and said to the dogs who were peeping out from the kitchen doorway, not feeling safe while the vacuum cleaner hose was snaking across the floor, "Not my business anyway."

She finished up her cleaning with a sigh. "A little of this goes a long way, kiddos," she said, passing the back of her hand over her forehead. "Can't see what my mother sees in it ... Let's go out!"

She stowed the cleaning things, to the dogs' great relief, and they set off for their daily walk. "We're not going to be too long," she told them as she picked up their pink and blue leads, "got a lesson later on - your wicked stepmother is becoming a dog trainer - thanks to you two!"

Jasper and Flora smiled in happy ignorance of what she'd said - except that they were going for a walk - their tongues were lolling and tails thumping as they set off through the garden. Tamsin was getting used to this new life, playing around with dogs all day - and getting paid for it some of the time!

It was only a few days later that she heard a taxi pull up outside the house, and she clambered up the steps - accompanied by two highly excited dogs - in time to help Robin carry his many bags down to the house, each bag being minutely inspected by the sniffer dogs. Robin's face looked odd, but not wanting to stare she waited till he was in the kitchen and she had the kettle on before studying his face.

"Oh!" she said with sudden understanding, "It's the mark of your snow goggles!"

Robin looked up, puzzled.

"You have a suntanned face, but white panda eyes - that's from your snow goggles, right?"

"Oh yes, indeed, that's so. Goggles! We get used to looking like this, don't you know?"

"So people will know where you've been for quite a while, till it wears off in our thinner sunshine."

"Once I get on the Hills again with these two," he nodded to Jasper and Flora who, after their initial excitement were now lying calmly on their beds. "But what's happened to them? Why aren't they racing about grabbing tea-towels and books in their mouths? Are they ill?"

"Remember you asked about training them? Well, I've been enjoying myself doing a bit of work with them," Tamsin explained. "You'll find them rather easier to walk, I think?"

"You mean I'll have to pull myself up the hill instead of them doing it for me?" he laughed. "I'll stow all this lot in my bedroom for now," he indicated his bags. You're off tomorrow, is that right?"

"Yes. I did what you suggested and got a bike, so I'll cycle into the sunset tomorrow - figuratively speaking, of course! I'll actually cycle the opposite direction, towards Great Malvern, and it'll be in the morning. While you're unpacking, I'll just finish my packing," and so saying she went off to her bedroom. After a glance at Robin, the two dogs padded after her.

Having packed all she could till tomorrow, she sat back on her bed and picked up one of her library books. She was quite absorbed in finding just how much exercise a puppy should get each day, when she heard a crash and a scream from the kitchen.

She leaped from her bed and ran to find Robin clawing at his shirt, now soaked through with steaming liquid.

"I thought I'd make myself some tinned soup," he gasped, and I managed to drop the pan and splash it all over me .."

"It's scalding - we need to get it off you at once!" and she quickly peeled the hot soupy shirt off him and dropped it in the sink. She found a clean towel and soaking it under the cold tap, wrung it out and started to mop Robin's shoulder and chest, Jasper and Flora happily licking up the splashes of soup on the floor. "Perhaps you should take a cool shower," she said. "You need to take the heat out of your skin before it blisters."

"You're right," he mumbled and wrapping the wet towel round his shoulders stumbled off towards the bathroom.

Tamsin heard the shower start up, and cleared up the mess in the kitchen, rinsing the shirt before dropping it in the washing machine. She thought of Robin's poor scalded body, his richly-tanned skin already angry and red ...

"Tanned skin!" she said quietly to the dogs. "His face has white goggle-marks, but his body is beautifully tanned! What's going on?"

At supper later that evening, Robin having stayed in the cool shower long enough to forestall much of the burning, but not entirely comfortable, Tamsin asked him some questions.

"I was thinking of writing a book myself one day," she began. "So how much can you expect in royalties from a publisher?" She hoped her leading question would definitely lead somewhere.

"Well, it all depends really. The more books you write the more they like it. My publisher is always nagging me for another book - a sequel."

"About the Arctic?"

"Yes, that's what they're after."

"And you won't write it?"

He looked up at her with two dots of red showing in his cheeks.

"Or is it that you *can't* write it?"

Robin sagged back in his chair, said "ouch" and leaned back more gingerly.

"You haven't been there, have you." Tamsin declared.

CHAPTER TEN

"You simply haven't been there. You left your skis behind, you didn't take lots of heavy food supplies, those strange phone calls, you're suntanned all over. I expect your suitcases contain Hawaiian shirts and tubes of sun cream."

Robin thumped his fist on the table. "Have you been snooping? I knew I should have chucked those dogs into a kennel somewhere instead of having someone to stay ..."

"No, really, I haven't - I wouldn't. It's just that over the last eight weeks I kept coming across things which just ... didn't add up."

"So you know. Are you going to blackmail me now?"

"No! Absolutely not! I'm just curious to know what's going on and, perhaps why. Really! I wish you no harm - no harm at all."

Robin slumped back in his chair again and sighed loudly. "The Azores," he said glumly. "Not Hawaii. The Azores."

"Why the pretence?" Tamsin asked softly.

"People think I'm brave. But I'm not. Not at all. It was fun the first time. Until one of the sledges disappeared in the night. A crevasse opened up and swallowed it. Gone. In a moment. Fortunately no-one was driving it, no dogs attached." He shifted his position painfully. "But it put the fear of God into me. I just ... couldn't go back. I suppose you could say I lost my nerve."

"But that's absolutely understandable! Anyone would surely see that? So why the subterfuge?"

"I'd already received an advance for the book, so I had to write the blessed thing. Then I became a minor celebrity round here. People wanted lectures, interviews, and the like. And I needed the money. What my parents had left me had just about run out." He got up and stared out of the window, at the sun just disappearing behind the Black Mountains. "I got enmeshed in the story. I was living a lie! I couldn't see how to get out of it!"

"So you kept giving lectures using your few old photos ..."

"I did. And living in the centre of England, people thought it was fun to have a resident Arctic explorer - though goodness knows, they have to live somewhere." He turned back from the window and ran his hand through his hair. "The public seemed to expect it. And it just got deeper and deeper ... I was able to enthuse about exploration still - I love the prospect of exploring a new place and finding out all about it, living in it, absorbing it."

"Just not the Arctic."

"Not the Arctic."

"So how was the Azores?" Tamsin asked brightly.

"Well, actually, you know - it's beautiful." Robin marched back to the table and sat down again. "It's a group of islands, bristling with active volcanoes. It's got lakes with thermal springs - a bit like Yellowstone in the States." Robin leaned forward in his enthusiasm, more animated than Tamsin had seen him before. "It's got a beautiful climate - lots of sunshine, plenty of scuba diving ..."

"Hence the suntan?"

Robin blushed and went on, "and plenty of rain too, so it's a very green island."

"Did you do any exploring there?"

"I did lots of trekking and island-hopping, studying the volcanic activity - there was a minor earthquake a few weeks ago - absolutely fascinating!"

"Then why on earth all this lying? Why not write books about the Azores? There's plenty of material there and, who knows, people may prefer lush green sunny images to endless pictures of snow blowing in a blizzard."

"You're right, of course. But I couldn't think how to do it - how to switch. My publisher is dead set on more snow, as you put it."

"Your publisher is not your publisher. They haven't published anything of yours for years! Find another!"

Robin chewed his lip thoughtfully. "Perhaps you're right ..."

Now Tamsin leant forward. "You have to find what your passion truly is, and follow that. You can see that what you love doing is exploring. You have an enquiring mind, you like collecting information, discovering things. You don't have to stay stuck in the same place you began! Life is a wonderful journey!"

Surprised at herself, she took a deep breath and sat back again, then went on more practically, "Your other book was called *Surviving in the Arctic by Renowned Explorer Robin Langley-Fortescue*. Now you have to think of an attractive title for your new area of exploration. I'm sure we can come up with something better."

"*Active volcanoes in the Azores ...*" Robin murmured.

"*When will the Azores erupt?* Something gripping like that?" Tamsin ventured. "Did you take many photos?"

"Hundreds! Thousands, I think. Plenty of material there."

And they fell to cooking up titles and subtitles for Robin's new book - both happily engaged - until Robin suddenly said, "But how am I going to own up? No-one will ever trust me again!"

"Don't tell 'em," replied Tamsin firmly. "What the mind doesn't know the heart doesn't grieve over. Just be excited about the new direction and they'll follow you. You can tell them this is your new secret venture - a surprise. People love to have a hero to follow. And you can be that hero."

"I wonder."

"And if people here don't like it, why not move to the islands? They sound brilliant. I'm sure Jasper and Flora would enjoy lolling about in the sunshine."

"Actually it's a maritime climate - like ours, only warmer. Never too hot," he spoke with animation.

"There you go! It would suit the dogs perfectly. You're so keen on this place, you've got all the knowledge - your enthusiasm will shine through. It must be awful having to pretend to enjoy the place you're talking about when it's somewhere you never want to go again!"

"It's been tough, I have to agree. Really uncomfortable. Always having to watch what I say in case I give the game away .."

"It's all over now. When are you going to start on the new book?"

"Do you know Tamsin, you've really given me a huge confidence boost! I've been so stuck in the past. I'll start straight away - tomorrow. You're a breath of fresh air. I can't thank you enough for opening my eyes. I .. I'm sorry I lost it just now."

Tamsin beamed back. "You're fine. You can't imagine how *my* eyes have been opened over the last couple of months. I'm moving into an exciting new phase of my life - and it's all thanks to you!"

"Really? Oh, I say! How? Tell me what you're going to do."

"Well, after the dogs chased a deer one day, and nearly fell into a quarry," Robin's eyes widened. "I decided I'd take them to classes. And I ended up in this awful place with a man shouting at everyone, terrorising the dogs .."

"Oh that place, up past the new housing estate?" Robin nodded. "I went there a couple of times. Didn't like it. I'm no angel, but it's not right to abuse dogs and bully them."

"You see, your heart is in the right place! Well I wasn't going to stay there, I can tell you. So I went to the Library and started learning about the modern way of training dogs - it's all super-friendly and kind, and it works!"

"And this is why Jass and Flora are being so good now?" Robin looked over to the kitchen where the dogs were sleeping.

"Well, they fled there when you thumped the table."

Robin blushed and rubbed his face with his hands, his white goggle-eyes showing over his tanned hands.

"Swimming goggles!" Tamsin cried out in realisation. Robin nodded and blushed further, and she decided to move on. "But yes - they can choose to misbehave and steal things, or they can choose not to and have more fun that way. No need to order them about. Yes - I know it sounds as if the lunatics are taking over the asylum - but really, they enjoy it all. I'd love to show you what I've taught them. I've even taught them some tricks!"

Hearing about Tamsin's new venture and how she'd started a new life in just a couple of months, Robin became enthusiastic for her future too. The evening had turned from a disaster into a scene of hope and warmth.

And a firm booking for more training for Jasper and Flora, who lifted their heads when they heard their names, sighed, and resumed their quiet snoring.

CHAPTER ELEVEN

And so Tamsin had left Robin the next day on very amicable terms. She was genuinely interested in what he would achieve, and she assured him that his secret was safe with her. She would never mention her discovery. In his turn he promised to get no more misleading postcards posted from strange places (his old guide in Norway had done that for him, thinking he was escaping from a tiresome girlfriend), and tentatively offered her a place to stay, should she wish to sample the delights of 'his' volcanic island.

But she had more pressing things to concern herself with!

Her new lodgings were perfect and would do well till she got herself established with a bit more income so she could get a permanent place.

"In Malvern?" asked Charity one day in The Cake Stop.

"Definitely in Malvern! I love this place."

Using her new skills, patience, kindness, and her instinctive responses to animals, she quickly resolved her landlady's dog's thieving. Dorothy was so pleased, and told her many friends at the Women's Institute and the church. More students for Tamsin!

Her business was building fast - surprisingly so, she confided to Charity.

"Nonsense, my dear," said Charity. "You're giving people what they want - of course they're beating a path to your door. And when you've got your classes rolling at the disco place, you'll be even more well-known."

"You know Charity, I had a lot of time to think while I was tramping the Hills. All that fresh air must have blown the cobwebs out of my head! When I was working in a shop, and that little office I was in for a while, it always felt wrong. It just wasn't me. I feel so much in accord with the world now."

"You're doing what you were born to do!"

"That's exactly how it feels." She put her mug down and said slowly, "I was living a lie. So many people do! And the more you stick in that lie, the worse it becomes. I'm so fortunate that I've found out what I should do - what my contribution to the world is!" She held up her hand. "I know that sounds arrogant .."

"Not arrogant, dear - realistic!"

"I like that! I really feel the importance of being true to oneself. And I feel that I am. I'm following my passion. I'm helping people. And I'm helping these lovely dogs," she added, reaching out a hand to fondle puppy Muffin's ear.

It was a few weeks later that Tamsin caused Charity's phone to buzz again one morning with a message summoning her to The Cake Stop. And when Charity arrived, she gasped with delight, for perched on Tamsin's lap was a puppy - a black and tan dog with white paws and muzzle and an expression of great curiosity.

"Oh my! Is that a collie?" she asked, as Muffin put her paws up on Tamsin's knee to meet the newcomer.

"She is! She's going to be quite big, judging by the size of her Mum."

"*Merveilleux! Encore un chiot!*" said a familiar voice as Jean-Philippe came over to admire the puppy.

After much gurgling and cooing over the puppy, including attention and indulgent smiles from the other customers at the nearby tables, Tamsin explained to Charity and Jean-Philippe, "I suddenly thought: whoever heard of a dog trainer who didn't have a dog? I will be getting my own place some time, but I just can't wait," she gazed adoringly at the pup on her lap. "Dorothy was delighted with the prospect of a puppy in the house - so I went ahead and found just what I wanted!"

"So the big question is, what's her name?"

Tamsin turned the puppy towards her and said, "What's your name, little dog?"

The puppy tilted her head comically, one ear almost up and the other flopped down.

"You see - she named herself - it's Quiz!" said Tamsin happily, her eyes shining.

"Quiz! That's perfect," said Charity.

"*C'est parfait!*" echoed Jean-Philippe. "And will you be celebrating her arrival with cake?"

"Absolutely - bring over your finest!" laughed Tamsin, so content with the beginnings of her new life.

Want to know what's next for Tamsin, her friends, and her dogs? Read the next book in the series for her latest exciting adventure!

https://mybook.to/SitStayMurder

^^^ Scan the code above or click here to read Book One *Sit, Stay, Murder!*

> **When Tamsin stumbles upon a suspicious death, can she expose the truth?**

Malvern Hills, in the heart of England. Tamsin Kernick loves life with her four-legged pals. Warm and kind, all the passionate dog trainer wants is to make her school a barking success. But she panics that her dream career is about to come crashing down when one of her human students is found after class in the car park stone-cold dead.

Frustrated when the police prove less than helpful, she takes home the victim's poor pet while worrying that cooling corpses could be bad for business. And teaming up with her yogi housemate and a handsome reporter to investigate, Tamsin fears an attack on yet another client means the villain is intent on continuing their diabolical deeds...

Can Tamsin and her tail-wagging faithfuls pull all their tricks out of the bag to collar a killer?

Sit, Stay, Murder! is the charming first book in the Tamsin Kernick English Cozy Mystery series. If you like good-hearted heroines, cute canines, and frisky fun, then you'll adore Lucy Emblem's delightful doggie-themed treat.

Read *Sit, Stay, Murder!* to sniff out clues today!

ALSO BY LUCY EMBLEM

Where it all began ..
https://urlgeni.us/Lucyemblemcozy

Sit, Stay, Murder! *
https://mybook.to/SitStayMurder

Ready, Aim, Woof! *
https://mybook.to/ReadyAimWoof

Down Dog! *
https://mybook.to/downdog

Barks, Bikes, and Bodies! *
https://mybook.to/BarksBikesBodies

Ma-ah, Ma-ah, Murder! *
https://mybook.to/TamsinKernickCozies

Snapped and Framed! *
https://mybook.to/SnappedFramed

Christmas Carols and Canine Capers! A Howling Good Christmas Mystery! *
https://mybook.to/Christmascozy

Game, Set, and Catch! *
https://mybook.to/GameSetCatch

A Howl Lot of Love and Lies!

https://mybook.to/HowlLotofLove

The Charity and Muffin English Cozy Mystery series
COMING SOON!

* Also available in Large Print

https://mybook.to/TamsinKernickCozies

ABOUT THE AUTHOR

From an early age I loved animals. From doing "showjumping" in the back garden with the long-suffering family pet - many years before Dog Agility was invented - I worked in the creative arts till I came back to my first love and qualified as a dog trainer.

Working for years with thousands of dogs and their owners - from every walk of life, I found that their fancies and foibles, their doings and their undoings, served to inspire this series of cozy mysteries.

While the varying characters weave their way through the books, some becoming established personnel in the stories, the stars of the show are the animals!

They don't have human powers. They don't need to. They have plenty of powers of their own, which need only patience and kindness to bring out and enjoy with them.

If you enjoyed this story, I would LOVE it if you could hop over to where you purchased your book and leave a brief review!

Lucy Emblem

facebook.com/lucyemblemcozies

instagram.com/lucyemblem

bookbub.com/authors/lucy-emblem